What is Space?

I0553980

One day, Linda and Nemo were pretending to be astronauts. Linda asked Nemo, 'If you could go anywhere, where would you go?'

'I would go to space!' replied Nemo, 'I would fly around among the stars and planets and I would see the earth from outer space!'

'That sounds exciting!' said Linda, 'I want to go to space too! But what is space?'

'Space is the area above the earth. It is far away, hundreds of kilometres away from where we are. It is even beyond the sky,' said Nemo.

'Wow,' said Linda, 'If we had a rocket, we could fly up to space!'

'Once you are in space, you can fly about without anything pulling you to the ground!' said Nemo.

'That is so cool!' said Linda, and pretended to fly around, 'Tell me more!'

'I wish I could see what space is like myself,' said Linda.

'I could show you, but you have to do as I say,' said Nemo.
She covered Linda's eyes and spun her around three times.

When Linda opened her eyes, she could not see anything. It was all dark. 'Where am I?' she asked.

'You are in space,' came Nemo's voice. 'There is no light in space. In space, it is dark all the time.' 'That's scary,' said Linda.

'The Sun, the Earth, the stars and all planets live in space,' said Nemo's voice.

'Wow!' said Linda, 'That means that we all live in space too!'

'Yes,' said Nemo's voice, 'And in space, no one can hear your voice either!'

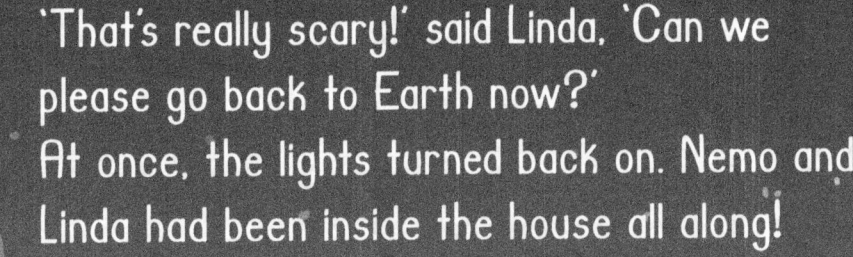

'That's really scary!' said Linda, 'Can we please go back to Earth now?'
At once, the lights turned back on. Nemo and Linda had been inside the house all along!

Linda was very happy to be back on Earth. And Nemo said, 'One day, they would travel in a rocket to space!'

The Earth

One day, Tiny's big sister Twinky bought a globe.

'This is called a globe,' said Twinky. 'A globe is a small model of the Earth!'

Tiny spun the globe round and round. 'But what is the Earth?' he asked Twinky.

'The planet we live on is called the Earth,' said Twinky, 'The Earth looks like a very, very big globe.'

'Wow!' said Tiny, 'Our Earth is so big!'

'The solid cover of the Earth is called land,' said Twinky. 'There are mountains and deserts and cities on the land.'

'Our houses are on land too!' said Tiny. He stamped his feet on the ground, happily.

'The Earth has water. All this water is in the lakes and rivers and seas,' said Twinky.

'And we all need water to drink and take baths!' said Tiny.

'The Earth has air too. We need air to breathe,' said Twinky.

'Yes, we do!' said Tiny. He clapped happily and took a deep breath of air.

'The Earth is the only planet with plants and animals on it,' said Twinky.

'Why is that?' asked Tiny.

'Because Earth is the only planet that has air and water. And nothing can live without air and water!' replied Twinky.

'Oh! We are so lucky to live on Earth!' said Tiny.

'Yes!' said Twinky, 'If we did not live on Earth, we would not be alive!' Twinky and Tiny did a happy little dance.

'We love our Earth! We love our Earth!' said Twinky and Tiny.

www.ingramcontent.com/pod-product-compliance
Lightning Source LLC
Chambersburg PA
CBHW081204170626
46813CB00009B/3317